COLIN
POLLEN

KID COMEX

WRITTEN AND ILLUSTRATED BY FIONN J. WILSON

To request permissions, contact the publisher at kid.comex@gmail.com

ISBN: 978 1716755798

To my dad

One day a kid named Colin was walking down the street and passed a mall.

Then he tripped on a strange looking stick and bruised his right knee.

And then a spec of pollen travelled from the strange stick to Colin's knee.

And transformed him into Colin Pollen!

Colin Pollen is a pollen monster that shoots pollen at people. He was turned this way by the pollen spec coming from the strange stick. It was all set up by the Super Peanut Villain because he wanted revenge for everyone laughing at him for being so small.

Luckily there was a cure D.O.T.S.

(Drops Organization That's Secret).
They fight allergies by giving medicine
like eyedrops to people who need it.

They went in their tank to help Colin, but their medicine was not strong enough.

They shot Colin Pollen with the secret formula hoping to bring him back to normal.

But it didn't work! And then Super Peanut Villain swooped down from his helicopter and grabbed Colin Pollen!

He brought him to his lair.

When D.O.T.S. came he was already making clones of Colin Pollen.

D.O.T.S. got their hose ready and they sprayed a stronger formula. This time it worked!

So, Colin Pollen transformed back into a kid.

And Super Peanut Villain went to jail, where he started thinking about his next plot…

THE END

I'LL BE BACK!!!

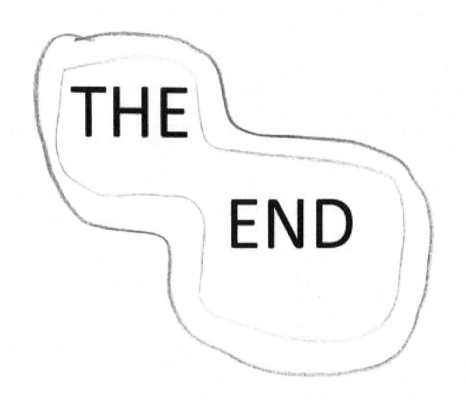

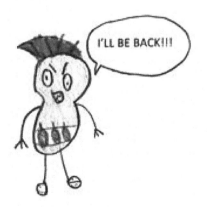

COLIN POLLEN

2

SNEAK PEAK!!!!!

IN THE MIDDLE OF SPRING . . .

. . .THE APOCALYPSE WILL BEGIN . .

.

. . . SUPER PEANUT VILLIAN WILL
RULE . . .

. . . UNTIL A HERO RISES!

About The Author

Fionn Wilson is a writer and illustrator. This is the very first book he has published. His favorite dinner is sausage, pasta, and corn. His favorite color is orange. He is allergic to pollen, dogs, cats, and several types of plants. He is nine years old (for now) and lives with his parents and his fish Harold and Franklin in Pennsylvania.

Lightning Source UK Ltd.
Milton Keynes UK
UKHW050641011021
391487UK00002B/170